THE WIZARD OF OZ

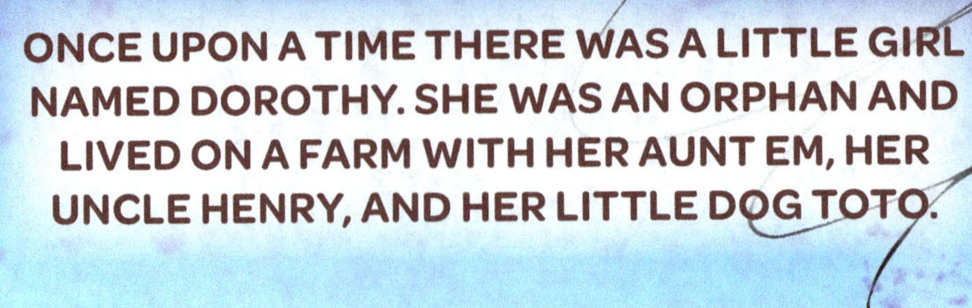

ONCE UPON A TIME THERE WAS A LITTLE GIRL NAMED DOROTHY. SHE WAS AN ORPHAN AND LIVED ON A FARM WITH HER AUNT EM, HER UNCLE HENRY, AND HER LITTLE DOG TOTO.

ONE DAY, A TORNADO PASSED THROUGH THE TOWN, AND DOROTHY TRIED TO HIDE IN HER ROOM. HOWEVER, THE STRONG WIND SWEPT THE HOUSE AWAY, TAKING HER AND HER DOG TO THE LAND OF OZ, A PLACE FULL OF FIELDS OF FLOWERS.

SUDDENLY, SOME MUNCHKINS APPEARED. DOROTHY ASKED FOR HELP TO GET BACK HOME, AND THEY SAID SHE WOULD NEED TO SPEAK WITH THE WIZARD OF OZ IN THE EMERALD CITY. THE LITTLE GIRL FOLLOWED THE ROAD AND, ALONG THE WAY, ENCOUNTERED A SCARECROW.

THE SCARECROW GREETED HER, AND SHE
TOLD HIM EVERYTHING THAT HAD HAPPENED.
SINCE THE SCARECROW WISHED TO HAVE A
BRAIN, HE DECIDED TO ACCOMPANY HER TO
ALSO ASK THE WIZARD OF OZ FOR HELP.

DOROTHY, TOTO, AND THE SCARECROW WERE WALKING WHEN THEY SPOTTED SOMETHING SHINING. AS THEY APPROACHED, THEY SAW THAT IT WAS A MAN MADE OF TIN. HE WAS RUSTY AND COULDN'T MOVE.

THE TIN MAN ASKED FOR HELP FROM DOROTHY, WHO PROMPTLY TOOK SOME OIL THAT WAS NEARBY AND APPLIED IT TO HIS JOINTS. IMMEDIATELY, THE TIN MAN STOOD UP.

UPON LEARNING THAT THE GIRL AND THE SCARECROW WERE GOING TO THE EMERALD CITY, THE TIN MAN DECIDED TO GO ALONG, AS HE WANTED TO ASK THE WIZARD OF OZ FOR A HEART.

DURING THE JOURNEY, THEY HEARD A ROAR, AND SUDDENLY, A LION APPEARED IN FRONT OF THEM. HOWEVER, JUST ONE BARK FROM TOTO WAS ENOUGH TO MAKE HIM CRY IN FEAR.

DOROTHY TOLD THE LION THAT THEY WERE ON THEIR WAY TO THE EMERALD CITY AND INVITED HIM TO JOIN THEM SO HE COULD ASK THE WIZARD OF OZ FOR COURAGE. THE LION AGREED IMMEDIATELY. HOWEVER, WHEN THEY LEAST EXPECTED IT, A VERY ANGRY TIGER APPEARED.

THE COWARDLY LION BEGAN TO TREMBLE,
BUT THE TIN MAN, WITH HIS AXE, MANAGED
TO SCARE AWAY THE ANIMAL.

AFTER A LONG WALK, DOROTHY AND HER FRIENDS FINALLY ARRIVED AT THE EMERALD CITY. THEY MANAGED TO ENTER THE CASTLE AND, UPON BEING TAKEN TO A ROOM, THEY CAME FACE TO FACE WITH A LARGE HEAD.

EVERYONE TOLD THEIR STORIES TO THE WIZARD OF OZ, WHO LISTENED ATTENTIVELY TO EACH ONE OF THEM.

THE ASSISTANT OF THE WIZARD OF OZ
FULFILLED ALL THEIR REQUESTS: THE
SCARECROW GAINED A BRAIN, THE TIN MAN
GOT A HEART.

THE LION TOOK A
MAGIC POTION
THAT MADE HIM
VERY BRAVE.

DOROTHY THEN BID FAREWELL TO THE SCARECROW, THE TIN MAN, AND THE LION. NEXT, THE ASSISTANT OF THE WIZARD OF OZ SPRINKLED MAGIC POWDER OVER HER AND TOTO, AND IN MOMENTS, THEY WERE BACK AT THE FARM.

WHEN THEY ARRIVED THERE, THEY WERE RECEIVED WITH MUCH LOVE AND JOY BY AUNT EM AND UNCLE HENRY, AND SO THEY ALL LIVED HAPPILY EVER AFTER.

THE END